HORRIBLE HISTORIES

HORRIBLE HISTORIES

TERRY DEARY

ILLUSTRATED BY
MARTIN BROWN

ON THE ROAD

READ ALL ABOUT THE NASTY BITS!

SCHOLASTIC

Published in the UK by Scholastic, 2023
1 London Bridge, London, SE1 9BG
Scholastic Ireland, 89E Lagan Road, Dublin Industrial Estate, Glasnevin, Dublin, D11 HP5F

SCHOLASTIC and associated logos are trademarks and/or
registered trademarks of Scholastic Inc.

Text © Terry Deary, 2023
Illustrations © Martin Brown, 2023

The right of Terry Deary and Martin Brown to be identified as the author and illustrator of this work has been asserted by them under the Copyright, Designs and Patents Act 1988.

ISBN 978 07023 2318 8

A CIP catalogue record for this book is available from the British Library.

Printed and bound in the UK by CPI Group (UK) Ltd, Croydon, CR0 4YY
Paper made from wood grown in sustainable forests and other controlled sources.

1 3 5 7 9 10 8 6 4 2

www.scholastic.co.uk

WHAT'S INSIDE?

Exclusive: Police report on the most calamitous car chase of the 1920s see page 54

FREE: Insert from the Chicago Herald on when Al Capone's gang impersonated the police see page 59

INTRODUCTION

History is horrible. For 250,000 years hideous humans have been inventing horrible things. Things like history lessons.

And even worse than history lessons are history teachers' jokes…

Apart from history lessons and schools, humans have invented truly horrible things – things that are still going on today. Things like murder. Back in 1888 Jack the Ripper became the most famous murderer in history.

IT'S KNIFE TO MEET YOU.

Jack was never caught. For the killers who were caught, the law invented machines that could execute. In the 1790s the French had the guillotine that beheaded thousands. They even sold a 70 cm children's toy that lopped off a dolly's head.

BRIGITTE THE BUTCHER

THE FINEST CHOPS IN FRANCE.

HEAD OFF TO OUR SHOPS NOW.

We're a cut above the rest

The guillotine was used to execute 10,000 people (plus countless dolls) when the French revolted in 1789, not to mention a famous French robber in 1956.

But 20 years BEFORE the guillotine was invented another Frenchman, Nicolas-Joseph Cugnot, invented a machine that went on to kill MILLIONS of people and still does. Over a million are killed by this machine every year and yet one and a half million are still being built every week. Each minute over a hundred are made.

What are these killing machines called?

No. I am thinking of transport.

No. In 2017 not a single person died in a commercial plane crash. On average, you could fly every day for 22,000 years before you have an accident.

Correct. How did you know that?

I GUESS I'M JUST A GENIUS

Now what you need is a book that tells all the gory stories about cars. A sort of horrible history of cars. Where can you find a book like that? In front of your nose maybe?

FAMOUS FIRSTS

1478 The Italian genius Leonardo da Vinci invents a car that will be a wonder to everyone in Italy. He draws it but never makes it. When modern mechanics try to build one it doesn't work very well because Leo didn't write instructions. And he's too dead to ask.

1672 Ferdinand Verbiest puts a steaming kettle on a trolley and the stream of steam pushes it along. He calls it a 'motor'. A new word.

1679 Denis Papin invents a safety valve that will allow steam engines to be built.

1769 Nicolas-Joseph Cugnot puts a steam engine on wheels that would carry four people at three kilometres an hour.

1771 Cugnot's steam car runs into a wall. He has invented the first car crash. Some stories say he was arrested.

1813 François Isaac de Rivaz fits a hydrogen and oxygen powered 'internal combustion' engine to a crude four-wheeled wagon and drove it 100 metres. The first car-like vehicle to be powered by an internal combustion engine.

1863 Étienne Lenoir from France drives his 'Hippomobile' further than any combustion engine before. It covers almost 18 km in less than three hours. Later a Hippomobile hearse carries dead bodies to the graveyard.

1896 Bridget Driscoll is killed by Arthur Edsall – the first pedestrian to die from a car accident. She is out for a stroll when the car zigzags down the road. It has room to pass but drives at her and runs over her head. The judge says, 'I hope such a thing will never happen again.' Some hope. Over one million people die on roads every year. A witness says, 'Edsall drove it at a reckless pace, in fact, like a fire engine. In fact, as fast as a horse can gallop.'

1899 The first car driver is killed. Edwin Sewell, aged 31, is driving a 6 horse power Daimler. A rear wheel collapses and the car hits a brick wall. Sewell dies on the spot. His passenger, Major Richer, is thrown from the vehicle and dies four days later in hospital.

1901 Connecticut in the USA has its first speed limits of 19 km an hour in towns. But it isn't the first. Around 250 years earlier New York City had a law that said:

PUBLIC NOTICE

No wagons, carts or sleighs shall be run, rode or driven at a gallop through the streets of New York. A fine of two pounds for those breaking the law.

1913 Henry Ford's car factory makes cars quickly and they are cheap. Thousands of people can own a car now. Hordes of Fords in fact.

1916 Cars are being made with windscreen wipers and rear-view mirrors.

1936 First diesel cars. It will take years to discover diesel engines pollute with soot. A cruel fuel.

1937 Volkswagen Works is founded by the Nazis to make what became the VW Beetle. They are short of workers, so they take them from their concentration camps. A Polish worker said:

I KNEW I WAS A SLAVE. THE FIRST DAYS IN THE CAR FACTORY MADE ME UNDERSTAND THAT I WAS JUST AN OBJECT. AN OBJECT THAT CAN WORK

Half the workers are women. When they have babies, the children often die from starvation. The Beetle car will go on to sell 23 million in the next 80 years.

1948 Ferdinand Porsche (1875–1951), the German car inventor, designed the VW Beetle. It did him no harm. In 1948 he sells his first Porsche sports car. They still sell over 300,000 every year.

WE DIDN'T USE SLAVE LABOUR THIS TIME

1959 The 'Car of the Century' is made. The Mini is skinny and tinny but ten million are made and that's many a Mini. They are still being sold.

1971 Ford starts selling the Pinto. It's often called the world's worst car. Its petrol tank can explode. Yet it's still on sale in 1980.

2018 Elaine Herzberg is the first person to be killed by a self-driving car.

2030 Selling petrol and diesel cars in the UK will end. Battery power now. Shocking news.

THE PAN MAN

Is your soup as thin as water? Yeuch.

In the 1670s Denis Papin (1647–1713) wanted

to find a way to make soup thicker. You could add marrow – the soft bit in the centre of bones. Getting the marrow out of the bones took too long. YOU try it. You need to be quickening the thickening. Dr Denis tried boiling the bones in a pan.

But Denis's pan was sealed so the steam couldn't get out. It built up pressure and really softened those bones. We call these pans 'pressure cookers'. Dr Den had a much cooler name for his hot pan. He called his invention…

Dr Den's clever invention had a valve on top. It let the steam out before the pan exploded.

A 'safety valve' was invented. Now inventors could build up steam to a high pressure WITHOUT their boiler exploding and covering them in scalding water. Now the steam engine was possible.

But Papin died in 1713 at the age of 66, poor and starving in London. He was buried in a grave without a headstone and nothing to remember him. His invention would change the world.

THE BRILLIANT BELGIAN

Ferdinand Verbiest (1623–88) was a priest from Flanders. In 1657 Verbiest sailed to China to preach the Christian religion. Thirty-five priests set out – only ten arrived. The others died of disease but Verbiest lived to preach in China.

Along came a new Chinese emperor who said it was a false religion. Verbiest and his friends were…

• Thrown into a filthy prison,

• Fastened to pegs in the walls so they couldn't stand or sit,

• Left for two months then told they would be strangled,

• Then told strangling was too kind – they would be chopped into pieces while still alive.

What happened? A miracle. An earthquake wrecked the prison and a bright star appeared in the sky. The Chinese thought this was a sign from their god. Verbiest was set free and became a great friend of the emperor and started inventing things.

In 1672, his greatest invention was a steam-powered car. A boiler made steam and the steam pushed a wheel that drove a 65 cm trolley. A model really, not a 'car' for passengers. But Verbiest came up with a new word…

Verbiest fell off a horse and died before he made a full-sized passenger trolley … a 'motor car'.

Now all it needed was someone to come along and put Papin's valve on Verbiest's 'motor' and make a high-power steam car. That man was a…

FANTASTIC FRENCHMAN

In 1769, along came another Frenchman, Nicolas-Joseph Cugnot. In 1769 the French army gave him the job of inventing a steam engine to pull cannons into battle. It ran at 3 km an hour and had to stop every 15 minutes to throw more logs into the boiler. Not a great success.

The king of France rewarded Cugnot with money, but in 1789 along came the French Revolution. The king lost his throne – not to mention his head.

FORGET THE CANNON TRACTOR – HOW ABOUT A GETAWAY CAR?

Cugnot ran away to Brussels but with no money he was almost starving. In 1804 he was invited back to Paris by the new emperor, Napoleon. A French hero. Hooray. A happy ending? Not really. Cugnot died soon after he came home. He ran out of steam.

THE FIRST CAR TRIP

Karl Benz (1844–1929) made the world's first petrol-engine car in 1885. But he wasn't sure it would go very far … so he never drove it more than a few kilometres.

His wife, Bertha Benz (1849–1944), was braver. In 1888 she decided to take her two sons, Eugen and Richard (aged 15 and 13), from their house in Mannheim to her hometown in Pforzheim.

'We're off to visit my mum, your granny,' she told her sons.

'But that's 105 kilometres,' the boys cried. 'No one has ever been that far in a car.' But they were as brave as Bertha and went along for the ride. She told no one – not even her husband Karl – where they were going.

As they puttered along, Bertha told the boys she had helped Karl Benz design the car.

'The leather brake linings? My idea. The fuel system? My idea.'

'*Mein Gott*, Mother, you are SO clever.'

'*Mein Gott*, I am,' she replied. 'But because I am a woman, I cannot have my name on my inventions. That is German law.'

There were no petrol stations – she had to stop to buy fuel from chemist shops along the way. The car stopped. Disaster? No. 'A blocked fuel line,' Bertha said and she cleaned the tube with her hat pin.

The car didn't have the power to climb some of the steepest hills. 'Get out and push, boys.' And so they did. They reached Pforzheim just after dark and drove home a few days later.

The news of her journey spread. Bertha Benz has made history and changed the world. The car was now not a useless little machine. People could be free to travel anywhere that there were roads.

Karl Benz became rich and famous, but he owed it all to his brave Bertha (and his pushing sons).

Karl wrote his own story and told of the days when everything seemed to be going wrong.

> *Only one person stuck with me in the small ship of life when it looked certain to sink. That was my wife, Bertha. Brave and stubborn, she raised new sails of hope in me.*

In 1900 a businessman in Germany, Emil Jellinek, put money into the Daimler car company and their cars were named after his daughter, Mercedes. When the company joined with Benz, the Mercedes Benz was born, and people still drive them.

But YOU know people should be driving the Bertha Benz not the Mercedes Jellinek.

THE FIRST POLICE CAR

In 1900 in Newcastle upon Tyne a horse was crashing around and hurting people on a drunken ride – the rider was drunk, not the horse.

A policeman went to arrest the rider, but the rider rode off. The officer of the law stopped a passing car – a Gladiator Voiturette – and set off after the happy horseman.

The car caught up to the horse, and the rider was arrested.

And the car driver? He was F.R. Goodwin who went on to be a famous racing driver.

AWFUL ACCIDENTS

There are famous people in history that everyone has heard of. People like Joan of Arc and Noah of Ark are famous. But cars don't care how famous you are. They will kill you anyway if you drive them daftly or get in the way of a ton of metal.

1 ANNIE OAKLEY (1860–1926)

Annie could stand on the back of a galloping horse

and shoot at targets. She even hit them. That is dangerous. The King of Germany, Kaiser Wilhelm, let her shoot a cigarette out of his mouth.

At one time Annie was said to be the most famous woman in the world.

• She would shoot a coin held by her husband between his finger and his thumb,

• she would shoot while riding,

• she could lay a rifle on her shoulder, shooting over her back, using a mirror.

Even when she was over 60 years old, she was setting records for shooting. She set off on a shooting tour and planned to star in a movie. She hit 100 clay targets in a row from 15 metres at age 62 in a 1922 shooting contest. Nothing could stop this wonderful woman … except a car, of course.

Annie and her husband were headed for their winter home on the coast in a huge luxury Cadillac car. It cost $5,090 at a time when $5,000 would buy you a farm.

They were speeding along when they passed another car and the driver let the tyres slip onto the grass at the side of the road. The Cadillac skidded into a ditch and turned over. Annie was trapped under a car that weighed more than two tons. She broke her hip and right ankle.

Annie had to wear a steel brace on her right leg and walk with crutches. Yet after ten months she was shooting again. She had to put down her crutches and stand on her good left leg, she hit pennies spun in the air six metres away. Several times she tossed five eggs at once into the air with her left hand and shot every one before it hit the ground.

Then another tragedy. Her dog – an English Setter called Dave, died.

SORRY, ANNIE, BUT DAVE'S DEAD

DON'T TELL ME. RUN OVER BY A CAR?

YOU GUESSED IT

After another year she was back breaking records. But the car crash injuries made her weaker and weaker. She died aged just 66.

2 ISADORA DUNCAN (1877–1927)

Isadora Duncan was one of the most famous women in the world in 1927.

Isadora often danced with no shoes and wore fluttery dresses and scarves. And it was the scarves that killed her … with a bit of help from a car.

Cars brought her more misery than anything. In 1913 her two small children, aged six and four, were in a car that plunged over a bridge and into the Seine in Paris. They both drowned.

Isadora herself was badly injured in car accidents in 1913 and 1924. She said she would never get in a car again. Wise person.

But did she learn her lesson? (You might guess the answer to that is, 'No', because her story is in a *Horrible Histories* book.) But she DID get in a car again. Unwise person. She wrote her life story and she said…

> *I am writing my story now because I am frightened that some quick accident might happen*

Amazing. She went to Nice on the south coast of France. Her end was in Nice but not nice.

A French driver was going to give the dancer a driving lesson in his Amilcar CGSS. She leaned back to enjoy her hair flowing in the sea breeze. Her long scarf also enjoyed flowing in the breeze. She called it her lucky scarf.

It caught round the back wheel. The driver didn't notice, and he set off at speed. Isadora's lucky scarf was pulled tight, and she was dragged backwards out of the car and under the rear wheels.

Isadora's neck was snapped, and she died. She was 50 years old.

3 JEAN BUGATTI (1909–39)

Ettore Bugatti built big and beautiful and fast cars. (For some reason they were called Bugatti cars).

His son, Jean, was a top racing driver and drove his dad's car at a French race known as the Le Mans 24-hour race.

Jean won in a Type 57 Bugatti tank-bodied racer. But he was sure he could make it go faster. So, he took the racer out on one of his usual test drive roads near the car factory.

Jean Bugatti sped around a bend and there, on the road, was a cyclist. The cyclist should not have been there and had pushed his way through the line of trees. Maybe he was trying to take a short cut. Jean was going too fast to stop. So, he swerved. He swerved into a tree and died.

We don't know why the tree didn't swerve, but it didn't.

Jean Bugatti was just 30 years old.

4 MARY WARD (1827–69)

Mary Ward was an expert on telescopes and stars, microscopes and insects. She was a writer and an artist. In fact, she was one of the most brilliant women Ireland has ever seen.

So, is she remembered for her great book, *A World of Wonders*?

No. She is remembered for being the first person to die in a car crash … sort of. The 'car' was powered by steam, not petrol. Mary was sitting high up at the front on a stool.

When the car went round a bend she fell off, under the wheels with rims of steel.

A doctor lived nearby and rushed to see if he could help. He couldn't. He said…

I saw the lady about two minutes after the accident happened. She was only just breathing. Her neck was broken, and her jawbone greatly fractured. She was bleeding a great deal from the ears and she died about one minute after I saw her

The steam car was broken up and buried under the courtyard of Birr Castle, Ireland, where the car's owner lived. That's what happened to death carriages in those days. No one said what happened to her stool.

5 ALBERT CAMUS (1913–60)

Albert was a French writer. He said some clever things and some odd things.

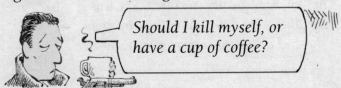

Should I kill myself, or have a cup of coffee?

He also said…

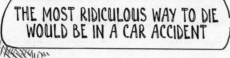

THE MOST RIDICULOUS WAY TO DIE WOULD BE IN A CAR ACCIDENT

On 4 January 1960, he was riding in the front passenger seat of a Facel Vega.

His friend Michel Gallimard was driving. They were heading home to Paris after a holiday. Gallimard's wife, Janine, and their 18-year-old daughter, Anne, were also in the car.

I COULD HAVE TAKEN THE TRAIN. I HAVE THE TICKET IN MY POCKET

THIS WILL BE QUICKER

But Albert never reached home. They got as far as Villeblevin, just over 100 km outside Paris, when Gallimard lost control of the car.

It swerved into a tree, killed Albert Camus and hurt Gallimard badly. Janine and Anne were not seriously injured. The car was destroyed.

The police were puzzled.

WE KNOW THE DRIVER HAD NOT BEEN SPEEDING, THE ROAD WAS STRAIGHT, AND THE PAVEMENT WAS NOT ICY OR EVEN WET

IT IS A MYSTERY

One writer said he had solved the mystery. He said that Albert Camus had been murdered because he upset the Russian secret service. A diary said...

> *I heard something very strange from the mouth of a man who knew lots of things. He said the Albert Camus accident was arranged by Russian spies. They damaged a tyre on the car using a clever gadget that made a hole in the wheel at speed.*

Killed by spies? Not likely. Camus planned to take the train. How did the assassins know he'd be in that car or that he would die when the other three lived?

But it's still a mystery why the car crashed.

DID YOU KNOW...?

Albert Camus was famous as a writer, but he almost had a career as a footballer instead. He played in goal for a French team until a disease ruined his health.

Albert Camus could save shots. He couldn't save himself.

CRAZY CARS

1 THE HORRENDOUS HELICA

In 1913 people had been flying in powered aeroplanes for over ten years. Propellors pulled them along far faster than cars.

Frenchman Marcel Leyat created aeroplanes and decided he could make cars go faster by giving them propellor power like his planes. He came up with the Helica.

BUY YOUR LEYAT HELICA

Let it PROPEL you into a new way of travel

160 km an hour

The French Flier for few francs

The Helica was fast. It had a top speed of 171 km/h (106 mph) in 1927, a terrifying speed for the time.

BUT propellors work by taking in air at the front and pushing it out behind. They also suck in anything that isn't fastened down: a lot of dust, stray pigeons, people walking along the pavement, small dogs, and cats.

The air it threw out behind was in the face of the driver – hot, dusty mincemeat.

Starting the car was a problem. You had to get out and pull a starter cord. When the engine was running you had to race to the seat and climb into the driving seat before it shot off on its own.

Leyat built 30 of the unique motors. He sold 23 then gave up.

2 THE HORSE-HEAD CARS

When railways were first invented people were worried the horses in the fields would be scared, kicking down fences and running through the villages. Some landowners tried to ban steam trains.

Sixty years after the first trains cars came along and people had the same worry about their gee-gees. So Uriah Smith of Michigan, USA, came up with the Horsey Horseless.

It had a horse's head on the front. (Don't worry it was a fake horse's head, not a sliced Suffolk Punch.)

Uriah had all the plans ready to go. Saddle-y he couldn't find anyone to build it for him. There was no one hoof thought it would work.

3 THE BMW ISETTA

This little car was made in
Italy in the 1950s. It had
two wheels at the front
and one at the back. A
little motorcycle engine
drove it along and two
people could just about
squeeze in. The door was at the front.

The car had no reverse gear. So, if you drove it
front-first into your garage, and got too close to the
rear wall, you couldn't open it and get out. You'd
have to wait until someone found you (or your
skeleton) and pushed you backwards.

4 THE PEEL P50

This was almost the smallest car in the world. One
person could fit in but there was no room for a
shopping bag or even your pet cat. Try to fit in a
moggy and it would say, 'Me? How?'

It had one wiper, one headlight and one door. There are only around 25 still left. If you can find one, then you could sell it for £150,000 because it is as rare as a smile on a history teacher's face.

In 1985 a smaller vehicle, the Sinclair C5, was launched. But it was a mix of pedal power and a battery. It had no roof, the battery could get you only 32 km, and it had a top speed of 24 km an hour. Was it a car or a bike? It probably leaves the Peel P50 as the smallest 'car'.

5 WOODEN WONDERS

If you heat up wood or coal it gives off a gas. Put a match to it and you have a fire. This gas was used for cooking and heating in the 1870s. Send that gas into a car engine and you have fuel. It's cheaper and cleaner than petrol.

In the Second World War (1939–45) it was difficult to get enough petrol in places like Britain. Enemy submarines surrounded the country and sank a lot of the ships carrying the precious oil.

Many cars were made to use wood gas to power them, and they worked well. Over a million vehicles in Europe were driven by wood gas.

The trouble is the gas had to be warmed for around ten minutes before a car engine could use it. But the biggest problem was the gas needed a large tank and it usually had to be carried in a tank on a trailer behind the car. It was heavy and clumsy.

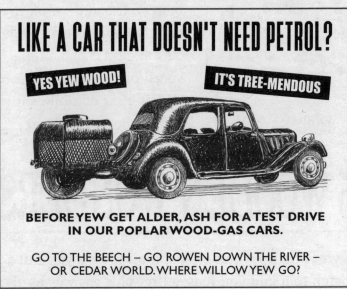

LIKE A CAR THAT DOESN'T NEED PETROL?

YES YEW WOOD!

IT'S TREE-MENDOUS

BEFORE YEW GET ALDER, ASH FOR A TEST DRIVE IN OUR POPLAR WOOD-GAS CARS.

GO TO THE BEECH – GO ROWEN DOWN THE RIVER – OR CEDAR WORLD. WHERE WILLOW YEW GO?

After the war drivers went back to petrol cars and you won't see wood-gas cars now. Wood you like to?

Coal gas was used to heat ovens and could also be used to power cars and buses and lorries. The problem was the gas had to be carried in a sort of balloon on top of the car. They were used in the

First World War (1914–18) and again in the Second World War (1939–45). But they looked very silly.

Getting under low bridges or keeping away from sharp-pecking parrots would be a problem.

Again, the gas-bag idea was forgotten after the wars ended.

DID YOU KNOW...?

The world's daftest car 'names' can be added to the world's daftest cars.

Here is a bottom five:

5 Mitsubishi Minica Lettuce (save the planet with this green car?)

4 Daihatsu Naked (drive it and you'd be a rude nude)

3 Subaru BRAT (for carrying nasty children)

2 Studebaker Dictator (for an even nastier ruler)

1 Mazda Bongo Friendee (bonkers friend more like)

And…

The Nissan Moco sounds all right unless you are Spanish. Moco means 'dried snot'. Who nose why they chose that name?

CWAINT CAR CWIZ

Test your teacher with these odd facts.

1 The word 'car' comes from the Latin word *currere* meaning what?
a) Hedgehog killer
b) Run quickly
c) Magic car-pet

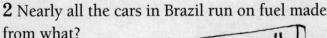

2 Nearly all the cars in Brazil run on fuel made from what?
a) Sugar cane
b) Oil
c) Cow poo

Smell POOTROL STATION

3 In 1900 how many American cars used petrol?
a) Three-quarters
b) Half
c) A quarter

4 In 2011 a Chinese farmer came across a barrier where he had to pay to use the road – a toll. He used fake number plates to dodge the payment. What happened to him?
a) He was forced to eat the cardboard number plates
b) He was banned from driving and had to use a bike
c) He went to prison for life

5 In 1912 a Renault Type CB Coupé de Ville sank in deep water. How did that happen?
a) It was on a bridge that collapsed
b) It was on the *Titanic* when it sank
c) An inventor was trying to make an 'amphibious' car that ran on land and water

6 In 1992 Michelle Knapp's parked car was smashed by something travelling at 265 km an hour. What?
a) A meteorite
b) A woman on a parachute
c) A tortoise that fell out of a plane

WHY DON'T I GET A PARACHUTE?

7 In 1909 Bert Scott's Ford Model T won a car race from the East Coast to the West Coast of the USA. But he cheated. How?

a) He put his car on a sledge to go down the Rocky Mountains

b) He put a new engine in his car halfway across – against the rules

c) He used rocket fuel to go faster

8 The Citroën Car company wanted to show how tough their car was. What did they do?

a) Drove the car at 96 km an hour into a giant bowl of custard

b) Drove their car off a cliff

c) Hit the car with a hammer

9 William Grover-Williams was a racing driver in the 1920s and 30s. How did he die?

a) He was testing a toy car when the wheels fell off.

b) He crashed and became the first Grand Prix driver to die in a race

c) He was arrested by the Nazis in the Second World War and shot for being a spy

10 The North Korean dictator, Kim Jong-un, has a Mercedes Limousine. But he also has a something special that follows him everywhere. What?

a) A mobile toilet

b) A kitchen

c) An ambulance

Answers

1b That old word *currere* also turned into the word 'carriage' (so get into your family car and ride like a lord) and 'chariot' (so, get in your car and ride like Boudica, chopping down everyone you don't like).

2a Sugar cane is turned into ethanol gas that powers cars. There's plenty of sugar in Brazil so it's a sweet way to drive. But cow poo can also be turned into a gas – methane – to drive cars. In one, five cows can give enough methane to take you around the world. And five cows would give you enough meat to eat on your poo-powered trip.

3c More than three in ten American cars used electric power and four out of ten cars used steam. Of course, you had to carry a lot of coal or wood and water if you wanted to go a long way in a steam car. In 2009 a steam car travelled at 238 km an hour across the Mojave Desert (California, USA). The boiler had the power of 1,500 kettles.

4c Tough but true

5b Cars and water don't go together very well. Neither do ships and icebergs.

6a The meteorite weighed over 12 kilos. Michelle heard the smash from her house and found the car crusher was still warm when she went to check the noise. The car was a Chevy Malibu and was worth $400. But it became so famous Michelle was paid $25,000 for it. Even better, she was paid $50,000 for the meteorite. People bought pieces of the rock and paid $125 a gram. The luckiest car smash ever?

7b The journey was 4,190 miles from New York to Seattle. It was meant to show how far a car could go. Bert Scott and his mechanic James Smith got as far as the Snoqualmie River. Then a rock under the snow smashed the axle. They worked for seven hours in the icy mountain winds to replace it. They won $2,000 … then had to hand it back because they had changed their engine. They were asked…

8b Citroën's Traction Avant cars were made very quickly in the factory. People said, 'They can not be safe'. (Except they said it in French.) The car tumbled over a few times. When the doors were opened the inside of the car wasn't damaged. Citroën went on to try safer crash testing in 1932.

9c William Grover-Williams was half-French and half-British. When the Nazis marched into France, Grover-Williams was needed for his skills to speak French. The British sent him into France to spy on the Nazi armies and wreck their plans. He was caught and shot.

10a He's just potty!

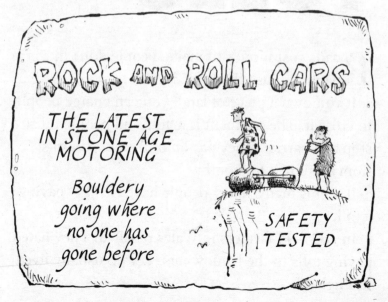

TERRIBLE TOLLS

Roads cost money to make. People don't like paying to use those roads.

If you own a piece of land, you can charge people to cross it. The payment is a 'toll' and people must stop at a barrier. They pay an officer who works from a cabin, a tollbooth.

It seems many, many people have HATED paying a toll.

In 1839–43 farmers in Wales rebelled. They hated paying tolls to the landowners ... who usually lived in England.

The farmers had to take their animals along the roads to market.

In the Bible a woman called Rebecca said, 'We must take over the gates of the people who hate us.' So, the rebels called themselves the Rebecca Rioters. And they dressed as women as a disguise.

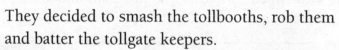

FEROCIOUS FEMALE DRESSES BEARDED MAN

Are YOU a Rebecca Rioter?
Come to Rhiannon's hair, make-up and nail bar
Hire your dresses and bonnets here

RIOTS-R-US
20 Front Street, Cardigan, Wales
(But we don't sell cardigans)

They decided to smash the tollbooths, rob them and batter the tollgate keepers.

They also started to wreck the workhouses where starving families were forced to live. They attacked the judges and police who tried to arrest them. When they came to arrest one of the leaders, Morgan Morgan, his daughter attacked a law officer … with a pot full of porridge.

• Sarah Williams was gatekeeper at the small village of Hendy. She was warned her gate would be destroyed that night, 10 September 1843. She refused to leave.

49

● Shots were heard. Sarah staggered to her neighbours the Thomas's house. She gasped, 'Dear, dear!' then fell dead in pools of her own blood.

● There were several gunshot wounds in her body. No one was caught or punished for her murder. Sarah was 75 years old.

Every tollgate in South Wales was smashed. The landowners agreed to cut the tolls, so the rioters won.

Tolls are still hated by some car drivers. And, just like the Chinese farmer in the Cwaint Car Cwiz Question 4, some people switch numberplates to dodge paying.

In the 2000s two tollgate keepers (also in China) were kidnapped by a driver so he could dodge paying 75p toll.

But at least the angry driver didn't shoot them.

Tolls live on. Sarah Williams didn't.

ROAD RAIDERS

In 1992 a thief stole a silver cup from a County Durham Museum and ran away. The police saw him waiting for his getaway transport … the next train to Newcastle. The train was late. The police saw him on the station platform…

'Stop there'? A daft order to give. The thief ran off again, over the railway lines and got away.

The police tracked him to his backup getaway vehicle ... the next bus to Newcastle. He didn't escape from the bus station this time.

BUS-TED

What the thief really needed was a car. Criminals have used cars to speed away from the scene of the crime for a long time.

1 THE GREAT CAR CHASE

In 1928 the London Police had crook-chasers called Leafs – short for Lea Francis 12/50 L Type. If they came upon a robber's getaway car, they had just one way to stop it ... they rammed it.

SET A LEAF TO CATCH A THIEF

WHAM!

Now imagine you are a robber … go on, just pretend. A little Lea Francis put an end to your four-wheel steal. What do you do NEXT time (when you get out of prison)?

I GET A FASTER CAR.

And that's what one gang did.

A VAUXHALL 30-98

AGREED. IT'S JUST THE SPEED WE NEED

Imagine you're a police officer and the Vauxhall leaves your Leaf behind by far? You guessed it. The police got faster cars. A need for speed that still goes on today. To beat the 30–98, London police bought the mighty Invicta 4.5 High-Chassis Tourer. The expert drivers were ace with the pace and known as … The Flying Squad.

The most famous Flying Squad driver was 'Jack' Frost and the most famous chase of the 1920s would have made an exciting movie. Frost's report could have looked like this …

LONDON POLICE REPORT

Date: 24 July 1929
Crime: robbery
Officer: PC 305 G.O. Frost

Report:

At 1 a.m. this morning Detective Constable Robert White of the Flying Squad called me at Scotland Yard to say he had seen three men we suspect of smash and grab raids.

I arrived in the Invicta and watched as they backed their Vauxhall towards Studd and Millington Tailors in Victoria Steet. Two of the suspects attached chains to the metal bars in front of the shop, planning to pull it away and break in. I drove towards them, and the men ran back to the car and drove off at high speed down Tothill Street. I followed with my partners, Inspector Ockey and Sergeant Ball. I caught the Vauxhall and pulled alongside as the inspector lowered the Police sign and Ball sounded the warning gong. The suspects ignored the order to stop.

Inspector Ockey jumped onto the door of the Vauxhall and grabbed the suspect driver round the neck but instead of slowing the car went faster as the driver called to his friends, 'Knock him off.'

One of the gang smashed the inspector on the head with an iron bar and the other struck his hand. Ockey fell into our path. We missed him and sped up Buckingham Palace Road at 130 km an hour. As the Vauxhall turned sharply into Ebury Street I rammed it side-on. The car turned on its side. The chase was over but two men with iron bars put up a fight. We arrested them and dragged them into Gerald Road Police Station. They were slightly injured.

Inspector Ockey has been found by a police patrol and is in hospital. The doctors say he will live. His thick hair probably saved his skull.

The villains went to prison for three to five years while the inspector was given a police medal for bravery. The Flying Squad became famous for these daring chases.

FLYING SQUAD BEATS LYING SQUAD
... USUALLY

The Flying Squad didn't always fly. In February 1946 the police heard of a plot to snatch a bank manager on his way home, take his keys and rob the bank. The squad dressed one of their officers as the bank manager then sat hidden in a car and waited for the villains to strike. The Spying Squad.

The gang struck. The policeman was smashed on the head and thrown into a van which drove away.

But his friends in the Flying Squad car didn't catch the robbers. Why not?

a) The police driver stopped at all the red traffic lights, but the robbers drove through them

b) The villains' van was powered by an aircraft engine and was too fast for them

c) The police car wouldn't start

Answer:

c) It was an icy February evening and the Freezing Squad car refused to start. The robbers went ahead with their plan to rob the bank and that was when they were caught. One man was copped putting the stolen keys in the door …

The policeman recovered … and got his watch back. We don't know what happened to the froze-in-snow and no-go car.

DID YOU KNOW...?

In 1934 the Head of the London Police, Hugh Trenchard, was angry when he heard 1,300 cars had been stolen in London the year before. He blamed the police car drivers for not being quick enough. He sent them to be trained by the world speed record holder, Malcolm Campbell. But he also did something mean to the drivers ... he cut their pay until they learned to drive fast and safe.

2 ST VALENTINE'S DAY MASSACRE

If policemen could pretend to be bank managers, then gangsters could pretend to be policemen. That's what happened in America in 1929.

In the 1920s America banned the sale of alcohol. People still wanted to drink it, so gangs started breaking the law to sell it and make a fortune.

But they had to protect their money with some pretty violent men. One of the most vicious gang leaders was Big Al Capone who sold booze in Chicago. And it didn't pay to upset Big Al.

A man who tried to steal Capone's business was 'Bugs' Moran. Al Capone set up a very special Valentine's Day gift for 'Bugs', then Al went on holiday to Florida.

The amazing thing about the story was the way it appeared in the newspapers the next day.

Chicago Herald

15 February 1929

COPS CHOP BUGS BOYS

Last night seven members of the 'Bugs' Moran gang died in a hail of machine-gun bullets. On St Valentine's Evening, last night, the men arrived at a warehouse in North Clark Street to wait for a truckload of stolen whiskey. But there was no whiskey – only death in a police trap.

A local resident, Andy Reiss, described the scene: 'I heard a truck door slam and looked out of my window opposite the warehouse. I saw two cops in uniform and two plain-clothed detectives get out of a police car. They ran into the warehouse. That's when I heard a sound like a pneumatic drill – I guess that was the machine gun. Then the two uniformed cops came out with their guns on two other men. It all went quiet for a while until we heard the guard dog begin to howl. It didn't stop so we went across to investigate.'

Reiss's neighbour, (who did not wish to give his name) said, 'The door was open, so we went in. It was like a slaughterhouse in there. There were seven bodies. The cops had just lined them up against the wall and blasted them. The blood was flooding over the floor and into the drain. The only sound was one guy moaning. We went and called for an ambulance, but it was too late for him. It's a bit of a shock to think the police can murder men in cold blood like that.'

The neighbour's wife added, 'Moran's gang stole booze from a police gang two weeks ago. I bet you this was their revenge.'

The police chief denies that Chicago police force had anything to do with the massacre.

Our reporter tracked down 'Bugs' Moran to his home today. Moran agreed the men were members of his gang but insisted, 'That was meant to be me in there. I stopped off for a cup of coffee so I was late. I saw the police run in and I escaped with my life. But I thought it was just an ordinary raid. I just can't believe the police would do this to my boys. We pay the cops too well. Only Capone kills like that.' The investigation continues.

Al Capone

'Bugs' Moran

The newspapers got some of the facts right but one important one wrong ... the killers were NOT the Chicago police. They were Al Capone's gang dressed up as police. They drove a Cadillac Sedan the same type and colour as Chicago police. They fooled their victims who lined up against the wall to be searched, and they fooled the witnesses.

Horrible Histories lesson:

Just because someone drives a police car doesn't mean they are police. If they are carrying a machine gun they are probably not.

The four killers were never punished by the law for the St Valentine's Day massacre. As usual the getaway cars were just too fast. But two of the killers died horribly anyway. These two, Anselmi and Scalise, agreed to turn on their boss Al Capone and kill him. Big Al heard about their plot and planned a suitable revenge.

Capone arranged a big dinner party where Anselmi and Scalise were the main guests. Al gave a speech and talked about how important it was to be loyal to your boss. Then he had Anselmi and Scalise tied to their chairs. He took out a baseball bat and, in front of his guests, battered the heads of the traitors till they were dead.

If that's not enough to put you off your dinner, what is?

DID YOU KNOW...?

Al Capone himself drove a 1928 Cadillac Town Sedan. Not a great car but his was made into one of the first ever armoured cars. It also had bulletproof glass windows.

No prizes for guessing why Capone wanted an armoured car. To fool his enemies –

and stay ahead of the police – his car was painted black and green like the city police cars. It had a police siren, flashing police lights, and a police radio hidden inside.

The windows had holes cut in them so a passenger could poke a machine gun out, shoot, kill and be driven off. It also had a cut-out in the floor so you could throw nails or oil onto the road to make it a hard car to follow.

Capone went to prison in 1931. The Cadillac Town Sedan was sold, and the story goes that it was used by US President Franklin Roosevelt. Except that is a big fat lie. He never did.

In 2020 Capone's car went on sale for $1 million but no one would buy it at that price.

Some of the bricks from the wall where the men were shot have been sold and the rest are kept in a gangster museum in Las Vegas, USA.

3 THE PROFESSOR'S PETROL PILL

For the first 140 years of their history, most cars have run on petrol. Petrol costs money. But what if you could make cars run on a special water?

Brilliant. Cheap and clean. That is what a German trickster Professor Enricht said he could make in 1916. Just add his secret pill to a bucket of water and run your car for pennies. He showed a few people how well it worked.

Of course, the companies who made petrol were shocked.

PROF'S PENNY-PETROL PANICS PRODUCERS

If cars could run on water no one would want their fuel any more. They offered to buy his secret. He was offered $100,000 in exchange for the secret formula in an envelope. But the Professor disappeared, and the paper in the envelope was blank.

People had SEEN a car run on water and the Professor's magic mixture. How did he do it?

A mixture of two chemicals, acetone and liquid acetylene can be added to water and make a car run.

Just two problems…

THE MAGIC WATER ROTS A CAR'S ENGINE VERY QUICKLY

HERE'S $100,000. FREE FUEL FOR LIFE

EXCEPT IT ISN'T 'FREE'. THE SECRET INGREDIENTS COST TEN TIMES AS MUCH AS PETROL

Professor Enricht was a trickster – a conman. He got away with it for a little while but then he tried to sell the idea of making car juice from soil. This time he was caught out. He ended up in jail for two years.

There are still people who want to rob you of your money. Now they call themselves 'Petrol Stations'.

4 FOUL FRENCH FIEVES

Citroën Traction Avant cars were so fast a famous gang of jewel robbers used them to escape from the police and became known as the Traction Avant Gang.

• Many of the gang had lived in France when the Germans marched in during the Second World War (1939–45). At first, they worked with the Germans but then they fought against them in secret armies – the French Resistance.

• After the war they joined with other crooks – and even crooked policemen – to start a life of thieving. Their Resistance machine guns were useful in bringing terror to the rich people of Paris.

• The leader was Pierre Loutrel (1916–46) who was so wild he was known as Peter the Mad. In a 1946 raid on a jewel shop he shot the American owner. But then had an accident and shot himself in the bladder. He died from the wound five days later. His gangster friends buried him in secret. The police found the grave three years later and dug him up.

• Abel Danos (1904–52) was the strong man of the gang. He was known as 'The Mammoth' because of his size. He was arrested after a shoot-out. Oddly he was sentenced to die by being shot by a firing squad.

• But the most vicious gangster was Émile 'Mimile' Buisson (1902–56) who was guilty of 30 murders and 100 robberies. He was sent to the guillotine to be executed.

• The Traction Avant Gang gave the idea of fast getaway cars to robbers in other countries. English robbers drove Jaguar Mark 1 saloon cars.

• American gangsters rolled up in their long black Cadillacs. It wasn't enough to be ruthless – you had to LOOK cool too.

5 MACHINE-GUN MENACES

Bonnie Parker met Clyde Barrow in Texas, USA, when she was 19 years old. Her husband was in jail for murder. Clyde Barrow was in the same jail for robbery. Bonnie Parker smuggled a gun into prison to help Clyde escape, but he was soon caught.

In 1932, Clyde was released and met up with Bonnie. They set off on a life of crime together. They stole a car and robbed banks across America. Then they turned to murder.

In 1934 they attacked a Texas prison to help their friends break out of jail. They used machine guns to shoot the guards – one guard died.

The couple stole a 1934 Ford V8 Deluxe four-door Sedan.

It was one of the fastest cars around at the time. Clyde even had the cheek to write to Henry Ford whose company made the cars.

Dear Sir,

*While I still have got breath in my lungs,
I will tell you what a dandy car you
make. I have drove Fords and nothing
else when I could get away with one.
Yours truly,*

Clyde Champion Barrow

(Clyde's real middle name was Chestnut. But a gangster called Chestnut is not really scary enough.)

The police just couldn't catch them. They gave up trying. Instead, they lay in wait for the murdering couple.

Bonnie and Clyde were tracked down to their hideout and the police hid in the bushes along a country road. When the killer couple appeared, the officers opened fire and slaughtered the couple in a hail of bullets.

The robbers were famous. Dead famous. They seemed to know they would end up that way.

Bonnie even wrote a poem about it – such a bad poem she deserved to be shot for it…

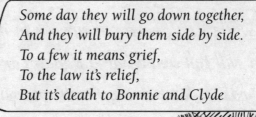

Some day they will go down together,
And they will bury them side by side.
To a few it means grief,
To the law it's relief,
But it's death to Bonnie and Clyde

To prove that the couple was dead, Bonnie and Clyde's bodies were put on show. Tens of thousands of visitors came to gawp.

But the car became famous too. The Ford V8 Deluxe Sedan had been stolen by the killers. The owner, Ruth Warren, wanted the holey car back. Why? Because nosy people would pay money to see it.

The bloodstained death car toured the country with a fairground show and in 1988 ended up in a gambling house in Nevada, USA. It is there now in a glass case.

• Visitors can see all 112 bullet holes in the body of the car.

• If you can stand it, you can even see Clyde's blood-soaked and ripped shirt.

• His sister signed it. (Well, she wanted to cash in on her famous dead brother too, didn't she?)

• As well as the real one, there are about six other Bonnie and Clyde death cars in museums across the US. They are all fakes, of course, but people still pay to see them.

That should be the end of Bonnie and Clyde's wicked lives. But is it? Visitors still go to see Bonnie and Clyde's Ford V8 Deluxe Sedan death car ninety years after they were killed.

They take photos of the car. But when they come to look at the photos later, what do they see? They see shadowy figures in the photos. Bonnie Parker? Clyde Barrow?

They also say that if you stand close to the car you can feel an unsettling spirit next to you.

The car has become famous as the most cursed and haunted car of all time. And speaking of haunted cars...

CURSED CARS

There are many tales about cars that are linked to evil or unusual happenings.

Horrible Histories warning: killing thirteen people is unlucky. You end up having to haunt a rusty wreck of a car.

There are other creepy car stories around the world, and we can learn from them.

1 THE BLACK VOLGA

In Russia in the 1960s people were disappearing from the streets of Russia. And wherever someone disappeared, there were witnesses who said a black Volga car was seen in the area. Was it a kidnapper? Was it a gang killing victims to sell their hearts, livers and kidneys for transplant? Was it a vampire-human draining children of their blood? Or nuns or priests or (some say) the Devil himself? Or was it Russian spies, snatching enemies of Russia and making them disappear?

The mystery was never solved.

Lesson: DON'T talk to anyone who stops beside you in a car ... ANY car.

2 THE VAUXHALL ASTRA

On 11 December 2002 the West Sussex Police had reports of a Vauxhall Astra going off the road near Burpham, West Sussex. After hours of searching,

they found a dark red Vauxhall Astra, nose-down in a ditch. But it was covered in weeds and cobwebs. The door was open, and the driver had crawled out to die … but that driver was almost a skeleton. Doctors said he'd been dead for five months. The driver turned out to be a robber who'd disappeared after escaping from the police. If the crash had happened five months before, then what had people seen crashing at Burpham? A ghostly replay of a deadly accident?

Lesson: don't try to speed away from the police. They'll get you dead or alive.

3 THE LINCOLN SS-100-X

On 22 November 1963, US President John Kennedy was riding in a blue Lincoln SS-100-X in Dallas, Texas. The car was altered in over 200 ways to suit the presidents who rode in it. One thing they forgot to add was bulletproof glass. An assassin, Lee Harvey Oswald, fired three shots at the open-topped car and killed the president who was sitting next to his wife. She was splashed with his blood.

The car was later fitted with bulletproof glass – a bit late. The car was cleaned and repainted black and used for 15 more years. It was then retired to the Henry Ford Museum in 1978. That's when stories started, saying someone dressed in grey was seen standing next to the car. It is usually seen in late November. President Kennedy was wearing a grey suit when he was shot.

Lesson: just because someone famous is shot in a car you don't just scrap it.

4 THE 1955 PORSCHE 550 SPYDER

James Dean was one of the most famous film actors of the 1950s. He also enjoyed racing fast cars. When he set off for a race in September 1955 he was driving his new Porsche 550 Spyder. A car in front made a sudden turn and Dean's Spyder crashed into it and he died. The car would bring nothing but bad luck after Dean's death.

The wreckage of the Spyder was bought by a man who wanted to sell bits of the car. As the wreck was being loaded onto a lorry, it fell onto a mechanic's leg. The new owner wanted to hide the Porsche but then lent it to a show to put people off fast driving. The garage it was stored in caught on fire. The Spyder was hardly damaged at all. When it went on show at last, it fell off the stand and broke a hip of a visitor.

Everyone who bought parts from the car had crashes, some with deaths. There are even tales about people getting hurt while handling the wreckage.

The car disappeared from a sealed car transporter and has not been seen since. There is a million-dollar reward for finding it. Dare you go on the treasure hunt for a cursed car?

Quick Quiz:
What was the name of the driver that James Dean crashed into?
a) Donald Duckpool
b) Donald Turnupseed
c) Donald Trump
Answer: (b)

DEAD DEAN DOWNED BY DON

5 THE GRAF & STIFT DEATH CAR

The First World War was fought from 1914 to 1918 and killed around 20 million people. And it was all the fault of a car.

A group of rebels from Serbia, known as the Black Hand gang, didn't like being ruled by Austria. So, they waited till the Austrian Archduke Franz Ferdinand came to Bosnia.

Gavrilo Princip was a Serbian Black Hand freedom fighter. This could be his story…

NUMBER 2, GABRINOVICS, NEARLY SUCCEEDED

I THREW MY BOMB AT FERDI'S CAR ... BUT FERDI PICKED IT UP THREW IT OUT

THE BOMB BLEW UP A FOLLOWING CAR AND INJURED EIGHT INNOCENT PEOPLE. OOOPS

NUMBER 2 SWALLOWED POISON AND JUMPED IN THE RIVER TO DROWN RATHER THAN BE CAPTURED

BUT THE CROWD DRAGGED ME OUT OF THE RIVER AND SAVED ME ... THEN THEY NEARLY BEAT ME TO DEATH

FERDI WENT TO THE TOWN HALL AND MADE A SPEECH. HE WAS IN REACH OF 3, 4, 5 AND 6. AND THEY...

ER ... DID NOTHING

FERDI HEADED FOR THE HOSPITAL TO VISIT THE BOMB VICTIMS. BUT, BY AN AMAZING CHANCE HIS DRIVER TOOK A WRONG TURNING THIS ROAD BROUGHT HIM STRAIGHT PAST NUMBER 7

ME

The first stone had been thrown. Austria declared war on Serbia and Germany helped Austria so Russia helped Serbia so France helped Russia. Germany marched through Belgium to get to France so Britain helped Belgium. It was a world war.

And so the First World War started. All because the Archduke's car stuttered to a stop in the wrong place at the wrong time.

The haunted death car

Duke Ferdi's death car was blood red – even before his blood was spilt. It went on to have other horrible happenings linked to it. It had 11 new owners and was linked to 13 more deaths … if you believe it. It is said…

• An Austrian general owned it, became ill and went to a mental health facility.

• One owner ran into two peasants, then into a tree within nine days. He was so upset he killed himself.

• A governor of Yugoslavia had four accidents. After one of them his arm had to be cut off.

• He sold the car to a friend who flipped the car over and was crushed.

• The same thing happened to a Swiss racing driver. He was thrown over a wall and broke his neck.

• A rich farmer owned it but broke down. As it was being towed it burst into life, smashed into the towing car and killed both drivers.

• A garage owner from Romania changed the colour to blue to change the luck. He then used the car to take five guests to a wedding. It spun and crashed into another car head on. Only one was left alive.

The Graf & Stift killer car is now in a museum in Vienna. Go and see it … if you dare?

DID YOU KNOW...?

A useless piece of Graf & Stift information for you to share with your teacher…

The Archduke's Graf & Stift death car STARTED the war. BUT it had a registration number A III 118. Some people read that as the date when the First World War ended with A(rmistice) 11/11/1918.

DID YOU KNOW...?

That it is a crime to drive around in a dirty car? But don't worry. That is only in Russia.

COME AND GET
YOUR CAR WASHED
AT YURI'S AUTO WASH

OR WE'LL CALL THE POLICE!

AWFUL FOR ANIMALS

A nimals do not read the Green Cross Code:

> **Before you cross the road…**
> **Think.**
> **Stop.**
> **Look and listen.**
> **Wait.**
> **Look and listen again.**
> **Arrive alive.**

Animals don't do any of those things, so they don't always 'arrive alive'. They don't arrive dead. They just don't arrive. Splatter, squidge, scrunch.

If a driver runs over a cat in Britain today, it's fine … except for the moggy and its owner of course. The laws say you only have to report dead dogs, horses and farm animals. Just as well the cat-killing drivers don't live in ancient Egypt where the punishment for killing a cat was death.

RIGHTLY SO

QUICK ANIMAL QUIZ

1 In Alaska it is against the law to carry a dog…
a) On the roof of a car
b) On a sledge behind a car

SLEIGH-HOUND

2 Dorothy Levitt, the first woman racing driver, went to race in France and was given a yappy Pomeranian dog, Dodo. How did she smuggle it back to England?
a) She drugged it and hid it in her car toolbox
b) She shaved it and put it in a pram and said it was her baby

3 The film star Jayne Mansfield (1933–67) died when her car ran under a lorry and sliced the roof off. Her children in the back seat survived. What didn't live?
a) Her pet monkey
b) Her pet dogs

4 In 2017 a bear started pressing the horn on a Honda car over and over again. Why?
a) Because it couldn't bear to see a deer cross the

road in front of a lorry
b) Because it was trapped inside the car

5 Minis can drive through safari parks but face a danger that other cars don't. What?
a) They are chased by lions wanting to eat them
b) Apes love the taste of their windscreen wipers and chew them off

Answers

1a) Odd to think the law must have been made because someone DID this? Were they barking mad?

2a) Dodo the dog lived. Back in the USA it went on all her journeys, cuddled up on the passenger seat under her fur coat. If you've seen the movie Wizard of Oz you'd know Dorothy owned a dog called Toto. This was Dorothy and Dodo. They never got to Oz.

3b) The car lost its roof – the dog lost its woof. Jayne's head was struck by the lorry as the car ran under it. It knocked her large blonde wig off her head into the road. For many years people thought the crash had knocked her head off. It hadn't. But the law was changed so lorries now had to have crash guards to stop cars sliding under them, they are often known as 'Mansfield bars'. No one named anything after her pet pooch.

4b) One night the bear had climbed into the car looking for food then pressed the button that locked the doors. It found the horn button and started pressing it till the owner turned up and set it free. It had ripped the car apart in its search. What a grizzly sight for the owner.

5a) No one knows why lions attack Minis. Some animal keepers think the lions see the little cars as prey. This has led to some very bad lion jokes. The mane ones are:

Did you roar with laughter?

DID YOU KNOW...?

A British driver was driving home with his window down. Someone threw something from a passing car through the open window. It smashed him in the face and broke his nose. What was the nose-smashing weapon? A frozen sausage. It is the only known case in the history of motor cars.

POWERFUL PEOPLE

T he world is full of normal people, but
sometimes it's the peculiar people who make
interesting things happen.

1 LUCY O'REILLY

In 1927 Lucy O'Reilly (1896–1952) became the first
woman Grand Prix racer when she drove in France.
She was twelfth in her Bugatti T37A. Later she
started to race off racetracks and roads in 'rallies'.

In the 1930s she set up her own racing team. At that time the monster Adolf Hitler ruled Germany and wanted to show the world how great his country was. He set up German teams known as Silver Arrows that started to beat the world. His minister Joseph Goebbels bragged:

OUR CARS ARE SWIFT AS GREYHOUNDS, TOUGH AS LEATHER, STRONG AS GERMAN STEEL

But Hitler didn't always win. At a Grand Prix in Pau, France in 1938, Lucy's Delahaye team entered.

Hitler and his Nazi party had begun to bring terror to Jewish people. So Lucy deliberately picked René Dreyfus to drive her fastest car. Dreyfus was Jewish.

Lucy's team gave Hitler such a beating he was furious. Beaten? And by a Jew? He wanted to make sure the race never happened.

Could YOU ever prove the Silver Arrows never lost that race? Hitler tried. His Gestapo bullies marched into the offices where the scores were kept.

BRING ME ALL THE RACE RESULTS. GO HOME AND NEVER COME BACK. WE WILL WRITE THE HISTORY NOW

In 1939 Hitler's Army marched into France at the start of the Second World War. Lucy O'Reilly's friends had to take the Delahaye race cars apart and hide the bits to stop the Nazis finding them and wrecking them.

But Hitler didn't manage to write history. The *Horrible Histories* truth is that brave Lucy O'Reilly was the woman who beat Adolf Hitler.

2 FERRUCCIO LAMBORGHINI (1916-93)

There are two great sports car makers, Ferrari and Lamborghini. The Italian Ferruccio Lamborghini made tractors. Very good tractors. But what he really loved was driving fast cars. The top cars in 1958 were Ferrari cars made by Enzo Ferrari and Lamborghini owned a few. He said:

THEY ARE GOOD, BUT THEY COULD BE BETTER. I SHALL MEET ENZO FERRARI AND TELL HIM HOW TO MAKE HIS FERRARI CARS BETTER

He told Ferrari:

YOUR CARS ARE RUBBISH. THEY ARE FINE FOR THE RACETRACK. THEY ARE TOO NOISY FOR THE ROADS. THE INSIDES ARE ROUGH. YOU DON'T LOOK AFTER CUSTOMERS AFTER YOU'VE SOLD YOUR CARS

Ferruccio Lamborghini said he could help Ferrari make better cars. Enzo was not amused.

YOU MAY BE ABLE TO DRIVE A TRACTOR BUT YOU WILL NEVER BE ABLE TO DRIVE A FERRARI PROPERLY. GO AWAY

That was when Lamborghini said:

I DECIDED TO BUILD THE PERFECT CAR. THE LAMBORGHINI. FERRARI NEVER SPOKE TO ME AGAIN. HE WAS A GREAT MAN, I KNOW, BUT IT WAS SO VERY EASY TO UPSET HIM

That story MAY be true. Or did Lamborghini make it up? It may be that Ferruccio Lamborghini just decided fast cars would make more money than tractors.

3 CHARLES KETTERING

In 1911 cars were started with a starting handle. (You turned it to turn the engine over.) Then the 'starter motor' was invented and is still used to this day. It was invented by Charles Kettering (1876–1958), an engineer who installed them for the first time on Cadillac cars. But WHY did he invent it?

The man who wrote Kettering's life story (his biography) told the tale.

In the summer of 1910, a woman was driving her car across the old Belle Isle Bridge in Detroit, when her engine stalled. A man who happened by just then stopped and offered to crank the woman's engine for her as it would take more strength. He was Byron J. Carter, maker of the vehicle called the Cartercar. As he turned the crank the engine kicked back and the flying crank broke Carter's jaw. Carter was not a young man, and the accident led to his death.

Now, it happened that Carter was a friend of Henry Leland, head man at Cadillac. Soon afterward, in Leland's office, Charles Kettering said that he thought it would

be possible to do away with the hand crank. That starter
was sometimes called the 'arm strong starter'.

Henry Leland was upset, and he said 'I'm sorry I ever
built a car. Those vicious cranks! I won't have Cadillacs
hurting people that way.' Kettering said he could
invent something to crank cars electrically. Leland
quickly agreed that Cadillac Cars would pay Kettering
to make an electric starter, which he did.

Starting handles led to many broken thumbs,
wrists and arms in their time and were still used
in the 1960s for when a car had a flat battery. Not
many starter handles were as deadly as the one that
clouted Carter.

Anger led to the Lamborghini. Sorrow led to the
starter motor. Or did it? The story may not be true.

HORRIBLE HISTORIES WARNING:

Was the story twisted to make a clumsy Carter look like a hero – a knight in shining armour to the rescue of a helpless maiden? A 'weak' woman looks as if she was to blame for his death.

YES ... Kettering invented the electric starter in 1910.

PROBABLY ... Byron Carter died from a starter handle accident, but it could have been his own car.

NO ... Carter didn't die in 1910. He died in 1908 ... that's what his gravestone says. A knight in ghostly armour? Cranky.

4 CHARLES GOODYEAR (1800–60)

Cartwheels had bands of iron around them – metal tyres. Very tough on the rotten rutted roads of the world. But on anything faster – like cars – they would shake you till your and your passengers' teeth sounded like a castanet orchestra.

What you needed was rubber tyres. People in Victorian times knew about rubber. It was used to make balls and make sheets waterproof. Not much else was done with it.

The trouble was it could get too hard or too soft. So early rubber tube tyres would grow sticky on a hot road; stones and rubbish would get stuck in them and soon make the tyres unusable.

Charles Goodyear spent ten years trying to make rubber useful. But he suffered. He…

• Owed so much money he was sent to prison,

• Mixed dangerous chemicals to make the rubber harder,

• Made such a stink from his experiments that the neighbours called the police,

• Fell ill from breathing in the chemicals and

• Sold his house and furniture to pay for more experiments.

At last – in 1839 – he mixed the chemical sulphur with the rubber. It didn't work until he spilled some on the top of his stove.

Would you believe it? Sulphur AND heating made rubber tough and hard. He had cracked the problem … just in time for cars to be invented and run – on rubber tyres.

Other people copied his discovery and made millions of dollars. One of these men was Charles Macintosh. Vulcan was the Roman god of fire, so Macintosh called the heat treatment 'vulcanisation'.

Goodyear died a poor man owing $200,000. His death was sad. He set off to see his dying daughter in New York. Some shock news killed him.

5 KING LEOPOLD OF BELGIUM

Rubber had been cheap because it wasn't much use. Goodyear made it useful. Now everyone wanted it and would do evil things to get it.

Julio César Arana had rubber tree farms on the borders of Peru and Colombia. He had a small army to help him and they:

• Captured indigenous people to work on the rubber plantations,

• Treated the workers like enslaved people a hundred years after the slave trade ended,

• Kept the workers starving and filthy, working long hours,

• Beat and tortured them if they didn't give Julio César Arana all he wanted and

• Bound and blindfolded rebels and blasted them between the legs with shotguns.

In twelve years, the number of indigenous people fell from over 30,000 to less than 8,000 while Arana made 3.5 million kilos of rubber and earned over $75 million.

Julio César Arana supplied the rubber, but the people who made the most money from the cruel trade were from Europe and North America.

In 1876, an English planter, Henry Wickham, collected 70,000 seeds from South America.

I CAN SEND THESE TO THE BRITISH PLANTERS IN ASIA. WE'LL HAVE OUR OWN RUBBER INDUSTRY AND KEEP ALL THE PROFITS

Rubber is made by making a cut in the bark of the rubber tree and letting the runny rubber flow. But not all of the British farmers in Asia were very bright. One planter grew hundreds of trees. When he discovered that balls of rubber were not hanging from their branches, he chopped them all down.

Cruel Congo 1

The rubber trade in Africa was set up by King Leopold of Belgium (1835–1909) and was savage.

King Leopold told the world they were freeing

the Africans from Arab–enslavers. In fact, being kidnapped to work for the Belgian bosses was worse than slavery.

• Men, women and children had to carry huge loads for the enslavers.

• A seven-year-old child would have to carry ten kilo loads all day through the steaming jungles.

• They had nothing to eat all day but a handful of rice and stinking dried fish.

A visitor reported…

I watched a file of poor devils, chained by the neck. There were about a hundred of them, trembling and fearful before the overseer, who strolled by whirling a whip. For each strong, healthy fellow there were many skeletons dried up like mummies, their skin worn out, damaged by deep scars, covered with bleeding wounds. No matter how fit they were, they all had to get on with the job.

The Africans of the Congo weren't slaves – they had a choice. They could either produce enough rubber for the rubber farms – or face the *chiquotte*, an especially cruel whip. Here's how it was made:

WHAT'S WHIPPING SOMEONE WITH A BIT OF DEAD HIPPO GOT TO DO WITH YOUR CAR? **LET'S FIND OUT!**

First, take a dead hippo and skin it.

Cut the skin into thin strips and leave to dry in the sun.

Twist the skin into a long sharp-edged corkscrew shape.

Use it as a whip on the victim's bare back.

WHY?

BECAUSE TYRES NEED RUBBER

• The sharp edges meant the whip cut into the victim's skin.

• A few blows would leave you scarred for life.

• Twenty-five lashes could knock you out.

• One hundred or more (quite a common punishment) would often kill you.

Finally, after all that, the sufferer was expected to pick himself (or herself) up and give a military salute.

You think you can refuse to work on the rubber farm? Fine … the planter's men will hold your wife and children prisoner until you do. Or, even nastier, your children could be thrown into the jungle and left to be eaten by the animals … or thrown on the plains to be baked to death by the scorching sun.

THAT was the price of tyres. Cruel slavery and an early death. Remember it when you look at the tyres of an old car. But the car is king.

Cruel Congo 2

Ziki was seven years old and lived in the Congo. He worked in a mine and carried rocks in and out of the tunnels … tunnels that were held up by rickety props. Like the other men, women and children in his father's mine he worked without a face mask or gloves.

DON'T KNOCK THE PROPS WITH YOUR TROLLEY, ZIKI, OR YOU'LL BRING THE WHOLE ROOF DOWN

I'LL BE CAREFUL

Ziki was working for £1.50 a day. He had never ridden in a car. His family were too poor to own one.

Children like Ziki suffered serious injuries, broken arms, legs and skulls, or smashed spines, crawling through tunnels or carrying heavy loads through the darkness.

But Ziki worked with no shoes and one morning he stepped on a stone and stumbled. His trolley hit a prop, the prop fell so the roof fell. The boy was buried alive and his family never found his body.

When was this?

a) 1922
b) 2022
c) 1822

Answer: (b)

Cobalt is needed to make car batteries and there is a lot to be found in the Congo. A lot of the mines are run by poor families who need the money. Now that cars are turning to battery power, the world needs more and more cobalt.

Just as Congo children suffered to produce rubber for car tyres over 120 years ago, Congo children today are suffering to make batteries.

THAT is the price of batteries. But the car is king.

RACING RISKS

As soon as cars started to move then someone wanted to make them go faster. THEN they wanted to show they were the fastest. And that meant racing against someone.

Racers took risks. The higher the speed the greater the risk and the greater the disaster. Racing driver Dorothy Levitt wrote…

Wonderful. One can hardly explain how racing feels. It is like flying through space. I never think of the danger. But I know it is always there. The slightest touch of the hand and the car swerves, and swerves are usually deadly.

In going at great speed, the hardest thing is to stay in the car. Half the time the wheels don't touch the ground at all, and when they do touch you must be ready to take the shock or else out you will go. It is far harder work to sit in the car than to ride a galloping horse over the jumps in a horse-race.

That was the thrill and the risk of racing.

1 FROZEN FIRST

The first car race in America was in 1895. A Chicago newspaper offered a prize to the winner. The racers had to drive the 88 km from Chicago to Evanston and back. The trouble was that when the race started so did a snowstorm. A horse-drawn snowplough didn't work very well.

Cars didn't have cosy heaters and snug roofs back then. The cars were slow, so the drivers faced an eight-hour drive – in the icy winds and snow.

• Two of the drivers collapsed with the cold.

• Others got stuck in snow drifts or skidded into one another.

• The winner won at a speed of just over 9 km an hour. (Today's Grand Prix racing cars have an average speed of over 257 km an hour).

• The runner-up, Oscar Mueller, fainted with the excitement and someone else had to drive his car to finish in second place.

• The winner was James Frank Duryea.

How did they cheer for him at the end? Maybe...

In a practice race Mueller had won because Duryea had swerved to miss a farmer's wagon and dived into a ditch.

DID YOU KNOW...?

In the 1920s there was no satnav to help you not to get lost. Instead, you could have your car fitted with a compass. You could follow the needle all the way to the North Pole.

2 FEMALE FIRST

In 1903 Dorothy Levitt became the first woman to race a car. She held the land speed record AND wrote books. She even held the water speed record.

The year before in 1902 she worked for the Napier Motor Company as a secretary. The chief salesman wanted her to learn to drive and help him sell cars. Leslie Callingham, a car salesman had the job of teaching Dorothy. He was not keen and said...

MISS LEVITT WEARS TOO MUCH SCENT, JANGLY BRACELETS, HUGE HATS, SILK STOCKINGS AND FAR TOO MANY PETTICOATS

He forgot to mention Dorothy always carried a Colt automatic gun.

In 1905 Dorothy and her dog Dodo drove a car from London to Liverpool and back, over 660 km, to set a new record for a woman driver. She didn't need the Colt automatic.

In 1906 she broke her own speed record at the Blackpool Speed Trials. She wrote…

I drove at 91 mph (146 kph). But I had a near escape as the front part of bonnet worked loose. I pulled up in time, before it blew back and beheaded me.

In 1910 she suddenly retired from driving and died twelve years later aged only forty. In her life, apart from breaking records, she…

• Was stopped for speeding in Hyde Park, London. The police said she was going 'at a terrific pace'. She was furious and said:

I WOULD LIKE TO DRIVE OVER EVERY POLICEMAN AND WISHED I HAD RUN OVER THE SERGEANT WHO STOPPED ME AND KILLED HIM

• Ran away from home when she was 20 because her parents tried to marry her off to a man they chose.

• Taught Queen Alexandra of Britain to drive as well as the princesses Louise, Victoria and Maud.

• Won the first law case about a car. A van driver had run into her.

But her greatest idea is something drivers still use today. The rear-view mirror. She wrote…

> Women drivers should carry a little mirror in a handy place so they may hold the mirror up from time to time to see behind while driving in traffic.

It was seven years before carmakers copied Dorothy's idea and fitted mirrors in cars.

DID YOU KNOW…?

In 2018 a woman was caught using the mirror to put on her make-up. She had no hands on the wheel. A van driver – a man – took a photo and split on her. It is against the law (if you are caught) and you can be fined £2,500 and banned. Four out of ten women say they've done it. Men were not asked.

That wasn't what Dorothy planned when she came up with the mirror idea.

3 THE FIRST RALLY

The year 1896 brought the first speeding fine. The British law said cars must not go faster than three km an hour and a servant with a red flag must walk in front to warn pedestrians.

Walter Arnold drove his German Benz car at eight miles an hour through Paddock Wood in Kent and there was no red flag ahead of him. The local policeman spotted him and gave chase – on his bicycle. He caught Arnold after eight km and the driver was fined one shilling (5p).

The law was daft. Later that year it was changed. No more red flags and speed limits went up to 22 km an hour.

I CAN'T GO THAT FAST. I'M JUST TWO-TYRED

Car drivers in Britain wanted to celebrate so they set up a road trip from London to Brighton in 1896.

Of course, Walter Arnold took part in his speedy Benz car. It began when a red flag was ripped in two. *Cccct.* Thirty-three motorists set off from London for the 87-km trip and 17 arrived in Brighton.

The London to Brighton Veteran Car Run still happens on the first Sunday in November. The rules include:

• Cars must be built before 1905,

• Top speed is 32 km an hour and

• It is not a race BUT a record is kept of the speeds of the cars.

In the 1896 run Léon Bollée arrived first in a car from his own factory. He took 3 hours 45 minutes which was an average speed of 22 km an hour.

Léon Bollée had an accident in 1911, never really got better, and died in 1913. But it was an aeroplane accident.

I SHOULD HAVE STUCK TO CARS

111

Émile Mayade came sixth. He only lived two more years before he collided with a runaway horse and cart, fell from his car and was crushed.

WAY TOO MUCH HORSEPOWER

4 MANGLING LE MANS

In 1923 a new car race began. It was held at Le Mans in northern France. The car that went the furthest in 24 hours would win. They went around a racetrack over and over again.

It was a test of speed, but cars also had to show they could keep going without breaking down … not so easy in 1923.

The race has led to many deaths. The first – sort of – was in 1925 when one of the drivers, André Guilbert, died before he even reached the track. His car was hit head-on by a van that was racing along at high speed on the wrong side of the road. The van driver lived.

Oddly the dangerous race made cars safer ... car makers learned from the Le Mans disasters and gave us better brakes, seat belts, better tyres and stronger bodies. Car racing started using crash barriers after the worst Le Mans disaster of all in 1955.

CAR CATASTROPHE

Eighty-three spectators have been killed and another 180 badly injured at the Le Mans 24 Hour Race.

An Austin-Healey slowed suddenly, and a fast Mercedes-Benz driven by Pierre Levegh ran into the back of him. Levegh's car shot into the air. It struck a wall, the driver was crushed to death and burning parts of the car flew into the watching crowd.

The cars raced on. The organizers did not want to stop the race because the crowds would all leave at once and block the roads. Those roads had to be kept clear for the ambulances to get in.

The race was won by British driver Mike Hawthorn in a Jaguar. He was seen drinking champagne and laughing when he got the trophy.

The French newspaper showed the photo of Hawthorn drinking champagne and gave him the headline…

CHEERS, MR HAWTHORN

They were being sarcastic.

But Mike Hawthorn had his own accident waiting to happen…

5 ROAD RACERS

Not all races happen on the racetracks of the world. Ever since cars were invented drivers have used the public roads to race one other.

It is against the law but only of you get caught. Or die, of course.

Mike Hawthorn retired from racing in 1958. Three months later in January 1959 he was driving along the A3 Guildford bypass in his Jaguar 3.4-litre saloon – the favourite getaway car of robbers.

He was doing about 130 km an hour when he overtook a Mercedes-Benz 300SL car driven by a friend, Rob Walker. On a right-hand bend he caught a 'Keep Left' bollard and lost control.

The Jaguar smacked into a Bedford lorry before shooting off the road and sliding sideways into a tree.

The tree was torn from the ground and sent Hawthorn into the back seat of the Jaguar.

Hawthorn died. His friend Rob Walker refused to tell police how fast they were going. Most people thought they were racing and, in 1988, Walker said it was true. A friendly policeman had told him back in 1959 not to say too much about racing at speed or he'd go to prison.

DID YOU KNOW...?

At the deadly 1955 Le Mans race, the MG car company ran some new models including the MGA.

One crashed, rolled and landed upside down, burning. The driver Dick Jacobs lived but never drove again. The other MGA came 12th. The MGA car went on to be one of the most popular sports cars of the 1950s.

The car was used by many police forces in Britain. Male officers drove white cars and female officers drove black cars.

In 2022 it was voted the most beautiful car ever.

AIN'T I GORGEOUS?

TKU 331

EPILOGUE

Cars have changed the world. Humans can go almost anywhere and travel a lot faster than they did on foot or on the back of a horse.

There are problems with cars. They don't kill people – careless drivers do that.

Maybe that will come to an end when cars drive themselves using a computer to 'think' instead of a dim human. They are called autonomous cars.

Even safe cars can cause a lot of damage to Earth. Their petrol and diesel engines put deadly gases into the air. They are blamed for making the planet grow hotter – global warming. Ice will melt, the seas will rise, and homes will go under water; deserts will grow bigger and people will starve to death.

Diesel cars may kill you even quicker. The gases that come out of the tailpipes will get into lungs and make people ill.

Electric cars seem to be the future. But as a wise

American actress, Alexandra Paul, said:

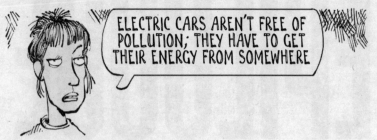

ELECTRIC CARS AREN'T FREE OF POLLUTION; THEY HAVE TO GET THEIR ENERGY FROM SOMEWHERE

She means making the electricity to power them still harms Earth.

AND ELECTRIC CARS STILL WEAR OUT THEIR TYRES ON ROADS. THE TINY BITS OF RUBBER ARE WASHED AWAY INTO RIVERS, THEN SEAS, TO HARM SEA LIFE

OI!

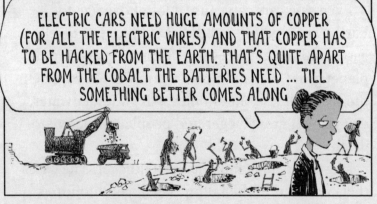

ELECTRIC CARS NEED HUGE AMOUNTS OF COPPER (FOR ALL THE ELECTRIC WIRES) AND THAT COPPER HAS TO BE HACKED FROM THE EARTH. THAT'S QUITE APART FROM THE COBALT THE BATTERIES NEED ... TILL SOMETHING BETTER COMES ALONG

Horse riders in 1800 didn't think horse riding would start to be out of date by 1900. Car drivers in 2000 didn't think petrol cars would be getting to the end of their road today. But they will.

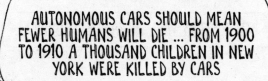 

AUTONOMOUS CARS SHOULD MEAN FEWER HUMANS WILL DIE ... FROM 1900 TO 1910 A THOUSAND CHILDREN IN NEW YORK WERE KILLED BY CARS

Louis Camille was the first New York child to suffer death by car. He was just two years old.

Cars have killed millions in their horrible history...

CRASHED

But cars themselves will die...

CRUSHED

You just have to feel sorry for the bank robbers when computer-cars take over.

GET AWAY CAR! WHERE ARE YOU TAKING ME?

TO THE POLICE STATION OF COURSE

The world gets safer and better…

BUT HISTORY WILL ALWAYS BE HORRIBLE

INTERESTING INDEX

Where will you find cow–poo power, haunted cars and sausage missiles in an index? In a Horrible Histories book, of course!

WHY NOT READ

INTRODUCTION

History can be horrible. It can be cruel, and it can be unfair. In stories like Cinderella or Red Riding Hood the goodies win in the end. The cunning, the greedy and the wicked are the losers.

That doesn't happen in history. In real life the goodies can die in misery and the baddies end up rich and famous.

In railway history the good, the bad and the daft often came to horrible ends. But say 'thank you' to them all.

Why? Because railways are one of the world's safest ways to travel. And that's because when the good, the bad and the daft made mistakes the railways changed. In the past 200 years railways builders have learned.

If you want to build a railway you need a book that tells you how NOT to do it. How NOT to be blown up, scalded, crushed or cremated.

PUFFING PIONEERS

If you ever get a poor school report, you can explain to your angry adult...

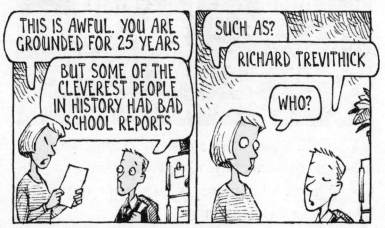

ROTTEN FOR RICHARD

Who? Richard Trevithick was a Cornish tin miner. And Richard had been a bad pupil at his school in Cornwall. His teacher wrote:

> Richard is a disobedient, slow, obstinate, spoiled boy, often absent and does not pay attention.

The tin mines needed steam pumps to keep the mines free of water. They used pumps made by James Watt, a Scottish inventor.

Watt had a 'patent' on his steam engine. That means no one could use his invention without paying him a lot of money. Watt became very rich. It was like a jackpot Watt.

Mine owners, like Richard Trevithick, were fed up with paying the Scot a lot. Richard decided to make his own steam engine. But it would be high pressure. He wouldn't have to pay Watt.

That made the Scot Watt hot. Watt a fuss he made.

HIGH PRESSURE ENGINES ARE DANGEROUS THERE MUST BE A LAW TO BAN THEM

LOW PRESSURE

If that law had been passed, then railways would have been stopped in their tracks. History would be different. The government refused to pass that law. Not what Watt wanted.

The 'disobedient, slow, obstinate' young Richard was clever at maths and inventing. He began to make his high-pressure engines. They were smaller and lighter than Watt's low-pressure steam pumps. So disobedient, slow, obstinate Richard tried putting one on wheels. His first steam carriage, The Puffing Devil, ran on a road, not rails, in Cornwall, on Christmas Eve 1801.

CHUFF CHUFF
JINGLE JINGLE

It ran well enough but lasted as long as his family Christmas turkey. The steam car had no steering. On 28 December, it ran into a ditch. A local person took up the story:

The engineers went off to the hotel and made merry with a roast goose and drinks. They had forgotten the engine, as its water boiled away, the iron became red hot and the wood frame burned to a cinder.

Richard went on to build a high-pressure engine to power a corn mill in London. A boy was left in charge but stopped the engine without letting the steam out. It exploded and killed four people.

Of course, Watt said what?

I TOLD YOU SO

STEPHENSON STEAM-AND-SON

George Stephenson worked on Watts engines in a Newcastle coal mine, pumping out water.

He watched horses pull coal trucks along rails. He knew rails were a brilliant idea.

In 1821 he said that...

A horse on a common road can pull one ton. A horse on an iron road can pull TEN tons.

George Stephenson didn't invent the high-pressure steam engine. But when he saw the high-pressure engine of Richard Trevithick he made it work a bit better. He built a locomotive called *Blutcher*. It was good enough to pull coal trucks. He boasted...

My locomotive Blutcher *is worth FIFTY horses.*

If you know your fifty-times table that means a locomotive on an iron road could pull 500 tons. That was a bit of a fib. *Blutcher* could pull 30 tons up a hill at 4mph.

A STEAM LOCOMOTIVE WAS WORTH THIRTY HORSES?

NO A HORSE ON AN IRON ROAD CAN PULL TEN TONS SO BLUTCHER WAS WORTH THREE HORSES

George THEN started to plan railway lines that joined up the coal mines to the seaports near Newcastle. Stephenson's steam locomotives would pull the coal to the ships where it could be sold all around the world.

Edward Pease, a Darlington merchant, saw how good the Newcastle railways were. He wanted a railway line like the Newcastle ones from the Durham coalfields to the port of Stockton. He paid Stephenson to build it, but Edward had a great dream...

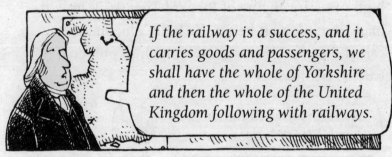

If the railway is a success, and it carries goods and passengers, we shall have the whole of Yorkshire and then the whole of the United Kingdom following with railways.

George Stephenson didn't 'invent' the railways – he took Pease's idea and made it work, just as he had with Trevithick's locomotive. George got all the praise...

GEORGE STEPHENSON, FATHER OF THE STEAM LOCOMOTIVE AND FATHER OF THE RAILWAYS

YOU ARE TOO KIND

Stephenson never said he was 'Father of the steam locomotive' – that was Trevithick. He never said he was 'Father of the Railways' – that was Pease. But George Stephenson never said he wasn't.

He WAS father of his son Robert Stephenson, and between them they went on to build railway lines all around the world.

Edward Pease thought his Darlington to Stockton line would be pulled by horses. But George told him...

Pease agreed. George planned the line while Robert built the locomotives. That first long railway was from the coal mines of Darlington to the seaport at Stockton. In 1825 that train carried something new ... people.

Crowds gathered to watch as George Stephenson's machine, *Locomotion No.1*, carrying 450 persons in 30 wagons at a speed of 15 miles (24km) per hour.

When the safety valve let out a screaming cloud of steam the crowds panicked. But *Locomotion* was not going to explode.

Around 450 people crowded into specially altered coal trucks and they set off. They had travelled a few hundred yards when one of the trucks came off the rails. It was lifted back on. Off they went for another few hundred yards and it happened again. The faulty truck was shunted off and a spectator was hurt.

The great train carried on for a few more miles ... until *Locomotion No.1* itself broke down. A fouled valve.

There were 40,000 people waiting in Stockton for the (late) train which rolled in at 3:45 p.m. The great men and women of Stockton headed for the town hall where a banquet went on till midnight. They drank 23 toasts that night.

Faulty Truck

Imagine that. The world's first passenger train was an hour late. It wouldn't happen today.

BUT DID LOCOMOTION NUMBER ONE *REALLY* PULL AS MUCH AS 50 HORSES? 500 TONS?

SHHH THE DARLINGTON TO STOCKTON TRAIN COULD PULL JUST 88 TONS ... BUT DON'T TELL ANYBODY

SHOCKING STEAM

James Watt said high-pressure steam was dangerous. In a way he was right. Use it carelessly and high-pressure steam can kill. But so can a match if you light it in the wrong place.

DO I HAVE MUCH PETROL IN MY TANK?

I'LL LIGHT A MATCH AND HAVE A LOOK...

BANG!

Steam engines, like matches, are safe if you use them properly.

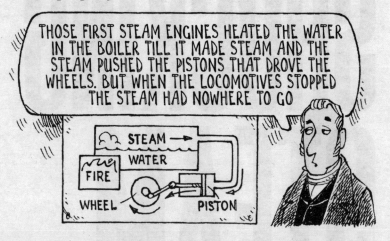

THOSE FIRST STEAM ENGINES HEATED THE WATER IN THE BOILER TILL IT MADE STEAM AND THE STEAM PUSHED THE PISTONS THAT DROVE THE WHEELS. BUT WHEN THE LOCOMOTIVES STOPPED THE STEAM HAD NOWHERE TO GO

STEAM →
WATER
FIRE
WHEEL ←
PISTON

Brunton's blast. Philadelphia, County Durham, England, 1815

One of the first steam locomotive explosions was the deadliest. Brunton's *Mechanical Traveller* was a steam engine with legs that pushed it along. He had it parked, steaming, near his house.

The *Mechanical Traveller* was so amazing the local people came out of their homes to wonder at it. But Brunton's boiler went bang. The driver was killed instantly (they usually were) while Brunton's nearby cottage was shattered. Mrs Brunton lived. Most of the victims were nosy neighbours.

Thirteen people died in this first disaster.

Safety sense

George Stephenson has a clever manager in his locomotive factory. The manager was called Timothy Hackworth. Hackworth came up with 'safety valves'.

But steam is power, steam is speed. Imagine you are a driver...

Dangerous drivers stopped the valve from working. It gave them more speed and power. Sometimes it worked, but sometimes...

SAFETY LAST

'Locomotion' loony. England, 1828

Everyone remembers *Locomotion* and the way it pulled the first passenger train in 1825. Hardly anybody remembers it was a killer. In 1828 the driver John Cree stopped *Locomotion* to take on water.

The gurgling and hissing of the water must have warned them that a disaster was coming. Timothy Hackworth said in his diary...

> ### JULY 1ST, 1828
> While John Cree was getting water at Aycliffe Lane with his assistant, Edward Turnbull, the engine exploded around one o'clock. He died on the 3rd at 3 o'clock in the morning.

And what happened to young assistant Edward Turnbull? Ed was scalded by the steam, but he survived with a face that was stained and scarred with soot-black speckles. He had to suffer bullying for the rest of his days.

Locomotion was treated a little more kindly. It was rebuilt.

Bottle blow. USA, 1831

Spotty Turnbull was a lucky fireman. The fireman on the American locomotive, *The Best Friend of Charleston*, was not so lucky.

Best Friend was a loco with a boiler that looked like a beer bottle. It could race along at 20 miles an hour. The Charleston Courier newspaper reported:

---

29 December 1830

The one hundred and forty-one persons flew on the wings of wind at the speed of fifteen to twenty-five miles per hour, defeating time and space, leaving all the world behind.

In 1831 the fireman had been shovelling coal all morning and stopped to eat his lunch as the boiler burbled away. The steam began to hiss and whistle (or wiss and histle) out of the safety valve. It really annoyed the fireman. So, he put a plank of wood on the safety valve ... and sat on it to finish his pie.

Steam could not get out of the top of the boiler so it blew apart the bottom. The driver was scalded but the fireman was blown into the air and died when he hit the ground.

I'VE BEEN BLOWN PIE HIGH

What 'ave we ear?
Wolverton, UK, 1850

In Wolverton, 26 March 1850 there was a similar problem. Engine 157 was left on a siding to build up steam. When the steam was up to pressure it started to escape through the safety valve ... safely. But the squealing steam started to annoy a workman's mate who was sitting near to the locomotive. He screwed down the safety valves as tightly as he could.

The boiler exploded. The workman had his ear blown off.

Express-o coffee.
Brighton, UK, 1853

The driver of tank engine No.10 had been warned not to let his engine build up more than 80 pounds of pressure. The driver of No.10 screwed down the safety valve till it reached 100 pounds. Of course, it exploded. The roof of the nearby station was mostly destroyed, and the driver was just as splattered. You want to know, WHY would he do such a thing?

The driver had climbed on to the engine boiler to heat a can of coffee over the steam ... the higher the pressure the hotter the coffee.

Putrid poetry.
Bromsgrove Station, UK, 1840

Thomas Scaife and Joseph Rutherford of *The Birmingham and Gloucester Railway* died when an engine boiler exploded. The killer locomotive was named *Surprise*.

The railway company was selling *Surprise* and the buyer was having a test-run. The wrecked engine was NOT sold. Surprise, surprise.

Scaife's headstone has a long and famous poem. It compares the dead man with a dead locomotive. How sweet.

RIP

My engine now is cold and still,
No water does my boiler fill;
My coal gives off its flame no more,
My days of usefulness are o'er.

My whistle, too, has lost its tone.
Its shrill and thrilling sounds are gone.
My valves are now thrown open wide,
My flanges all refuse to guide.

My clacks, also though once so strong,
Refuse to aid the busy throng.
Life's railway's o'er, each station's past,
In death I'm stopped and rest at last.

His clacks are gone? Like a dead duck ... whose quacks are gone.

Legs and logs. Harlem Railroad, New York, USA, 1839

You may not be killed by a blast, but you could live to have horrible nightmares for life.

A New York locomotive came off the rails then exploded. Workers arrived to put it back on the track. The report said...

The chief engineer was blown to pieces – his legs went into Union Park, his arms onto a pile of logs on the other side of the avenue, and his head was split in two parts. His abdomen was also burst and his intestines scattered over the road.

Moscow mess. Manchester, UK, 1858

A new locomotive was built in Manchester for the Russian railways. It exploded as it was tested. Three boiler-makers were killed. A young worker had been sent off to get a new tool from the shed next door. Lucky boy.

He heard the roar and looked at the scene of blast. He found body parts scattered around. These included a set of false teeth, a boot with a foot in it. Boilermaker James Carmichael was blown 70 metres over a canal, trailing guts until he smashed into a wall.

The mess that was left was stuck to the wall. A badly made boiler plate was blamed.

The luckiest – OR unluckiest – victim of that Manchester explosion had to be Thomas Forsyth. Tom had been hit by the first train to run on the Liverpool to Manchester service in 1829. He had a leg amputated and replaced with a cork one.

Thomas lived almost 30 years until that Russian locomotive blew up. He suffered a deep wound to his forehead through which his brains seeped out. A piece of iron had killed him instantly.

TERRY DEARY

Terry Deary was born at a very early age, so long ago he can't remember. But his mother, who was there at the time, says he was born in Sunderland, north-east England, in 1946 – so it's not true that he writes all *Horrible Histories* from memory. At school he was a horrible child only interested in playing football and giving teachers a hard time. His history lessons were so boring and so badly taught, that he learned to loathe the subject. *Horrible Histories* is his revenge.

MARTIN BROWN

M artin Brown was born in Melbourne, on the proper side of the world. Ever since he can remember he's been drawing. His dad used to bring back huge sheets of paper from work and Martin would fill them with doodles and little figures. Then, quite suddenly, with food and water, he grew up, moved to the UK and found work doing what he's always wanted to do: drawing doodles and little figures.

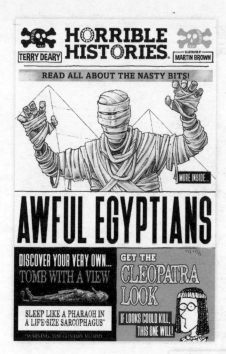

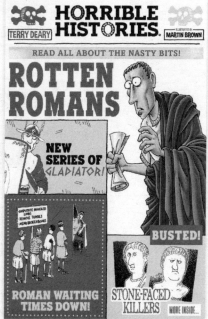

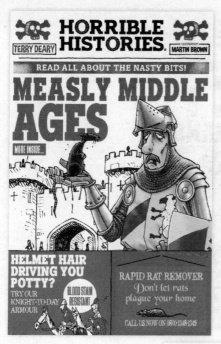

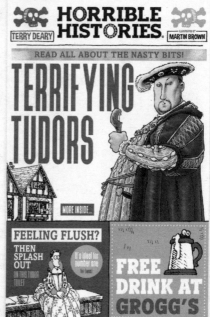

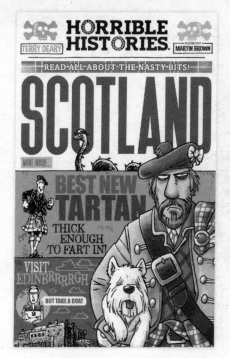

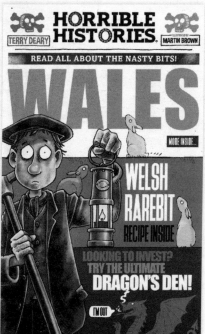

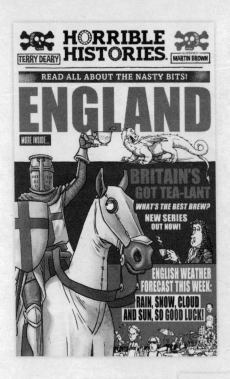

HORRIBLE HISTORIES.

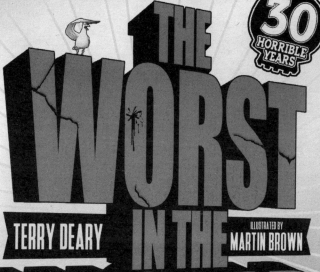

30 HORRIBLE YEARS

THE WORST IN THE WORLD

TERRY DEARY

ILLUSTRATED BY
MARTIN BROWN

I'M OFF!

☠ THE BEST WORST BITS OF HISTORY ☠